This edition published in Great Britain 2019 by Dean,
an imprint of Egmont UK Ltd
The Yellow Building, 1 Nicholas Road, London, W11 4AN
www.egmont.co.uk

ISBN 978 0 6035 7757 4
70623/002
Printed in China

BABAR AT HOME

JEAN DE BRUNHOFF

DEAN

One morning Babar said to Cornelius,
"Old friend and comrade
in good times and in bad,
listen to the happy news I have to tell:
Celeste, my wife,
has just told me that we are soon going to have a baby.
Take that new hat off the stool —
it is a present from me.
Take also the scroll, which is a message
I have written to my people, and proclaim it
to the citizens of Celesteville."

After congratulating Babar and thanking him
Cornelius went to put on his robes of state.
He ordered the drums to be beaten
in front of the railings of the Royal Palace.

Then he slowly unrolled the King's Proclamation,
and, having put on his spectacles, read it in a loud voice.
The elephants, running up in great numbers,
listened respectfully.

B

Beloved and loyal subjects,

Do not be frightened when
you hear a cannon fired.
It will not be a sign that
we are at war again.
It will simply mean that
in the Royal Palace a baby
has been born, the child
of your King and Queen.
In this way you will all
hear at once of the happy
event.
Long live the future
mother,
Your Queen Celeste!

Babar

Here, reproduced exactly, is Babar's message,
which Cornelius proclaimed.

Then Babar tried to read,
but his thoughts were elsewhere.
He tried to write,
but his thoughts were elsewhere.
He thought of his wife and of
the baby who was going to be born.
Would it be beautiful and strong?
How slowly time goes when one is waiting
for a longed-for event.

Celeste advised him to take a bicycle ride as a
means of changing his thoughts.
Babar agreed.
When he had ridden several miles,
he found a pleasant spot where he sat down
on the grass and looked at the view. Before
him stood Celesteville with the Fort of St. John.
"It is from there," he said to himself,
"that the cannon will be fired."

Just at that moment —
Boom!
Babar heard the cannon fired.
"There it is," he thought.
"How unfortunate that I have missed the event!"
Jumping on his bicycle he tore home at top speed.

On the roof of the tower
the Captain of the King's Artillery
himself saw that the orders he
had received by telephone
were carried out.
One cannon shot was fired —
then a second — then a third.

On the terrace-walk the elephants
began to assemble and talk.
King Babar had not spoken
of more than one cannon shot.
Why had the artillery fired three shots?
Cornelius himself could not understand it.

Babar arrived home
breathless after his speedy ride.
He also had heard the three shots.
Running upstairs four steps at a time,
he burst into Celeste's room;
with joy he embraced his wife.

She smiled at him,
and showed him
three baby elephants.
Everything was explained:
one cannon-shot for one baby,
three babies – three shots.
But what a surprise when one is
expecting one baby all of a sudden to find three!
The Old Lady held one, the nurse the other two.
Arthur and Zephir were very excited. Babar let them take a
peep at the new babies. On tip-toe they approached.
"Oh! how small it is!" said Zephir.
"And how pretty!" added Arthur,
admiring the baby in the cradle.
Celeste had only got one cradle
so the nurse quickly made
another out of a basket,
a napkin, and an umbrella.
It was a bit crude but
the babies were warm
and sheltered.

Then the babies were taken into the garden,
where they slept in a huge pram.
Babar and Celeste were congratulated by their friends,
each of whom bought a present.

Poutifour and his wife brought fruits from their
orchard, hens brought eggs, the gardener flowers.
The pastry-cooks brought a large cake, and
Cornelius three silver rattles.

Babar and Celeste had to think of three names
for their babies. Before they arrived
they had thought of several: Pom, Pat, Peter,
Julius, John, Jack, Alexander, Emile, Baptiste.
Alexander was not bad,
but what if the baby were a girl?
Juliette, Virginia, or . . .
"We must now decide," said Celeste to Babar.
"I should like our daughter to be called Flora."
"So should I," said Babar.
"And I think we might call the
two boys Pom and Alexander."
After they had repeated several times
"Pom, Flora and Alexander,"
Babar and Celeste cried,
"Good! We will decide on these names."

Every week Dr. Capoulosse weighed the
babies carefully in his big scales.
One day he said to Celeste:
"Oh Queen, the babies are not growing fast enough.
Every day you must give each of them, in addition to their
usual feed, six bottles of cow's milk and in each bottle
you must put a table-spoonful of honey.
The babies soon grew used to their bottles.
Arthur and Zephir loved to watch them drink.
The greediest and biggest was Pom
(the one Celeste is holding).
He cried very time
he finished his bottle.

19

1

Flora was a good girl.
She played with the
rattle that Cornelius
had given her.

2

She shook it about
with her trunk.
What a pretty noise
it made.

3

She put it
in her mouth
and sucked it.
It was lovely.

4

Suddenly,
she did not know how,
in one gulp
she swallowed it.

5

She choked
and grew purple
and her trunk trembled!
Celeste ran to her.

6

She seized her
and shook her, head
downwards. The rattle
would not come out.

7

Happily, Zephir
was able to
get it out
with his hand.

8

Flora was saved!
But she cried very
hard and her
mother comforted her.

Soon the children began to play in
their large sunny nursery.
Often Babar came to play with them.
Sometimes he sat Pom on his trunk and
jumped up and down.
This is the game of Hop-the-Trunk.

Cornelius fixed up a swing at the end
of his tusks for Alexander,
and Arthur gently pushed him.
The two boys learnt to walk before their sister,
but Flora is learning fast.
Already she can start off by herself.

When the children were dressed,
the nurse took them out in their big perambulator.
They were still too young to walk far.
One day the nurse said to Arthur:
"It's colder than I thought.
The house is not far away;
I will run and fetch the babies' jerseys
so that they won't catch cold.
Will you look after them while I am gone?"
Feeling very proud, Arthur pushed
the pram to and fro,

twenty yards forward and twenty yards back.
He was careful, avoiding all the stones.
All at once he heard the soldiers.
Letting go the handle, he turned to look at them.
The road sloped gently at that point,
and the pram began
to roll away by itself.
Pom, Flora and Alexander
thought this great fun,
but Arthur was frightened and ran after them.
The slope became gradually steeper.

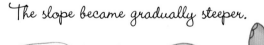

The pram ran faster and faster.

The children began to be frightened.

Arthur ran after them as hard as he could.

The nurse, returning with the jerseys,

ran too, with her heart in her mouth.

The danger grew great.

A little lower down, the road turned and

ran along the side of a deep ravine.

If the pram were not stopped before the turn,

it would turn straight on and then . . .

an accident!

Martha the tortoise,

who was walking nearby, realised the situation.

She ran as fast as her little legs could go,

and threw herself in front of the wheels
of the pram just as it was about to
fall over the precipice.
The pram, stopped suddenly when going at full speed,
rocked violently and nearly turned over.
Pom and Flora were thrown into the
hood and caught there,
but poor Alexander was shot out.
The nurse shrieked and the rabbit ran away.

27

28

Mr. and
Mrs. Squirrel
also heard the nurse's shriek
and, next moment,
the noise of leaves
crackling and branches
breaking just above
them, to the left.
Both together they
looked up and
saw the head
of a little elephant,
who cried:
"Mummy!
Alessander has gone bump!
Mummy!
Alessander has gone bump!"

29

"Courage, little elephant!
Don't let go!
We are coming!"
cried the squirrels.
"Swing yourself a little
and try to put your foot
on the thick branch.
That's right!
Don't be afraid!
We'll help you!"

The plan having succeeded,
Mr. Squirrel continued:
"Hold tight to my tail,
and, to balance yourself,
wave your great big ears about.
Take care! Follow me.
You shall have a
rest when you are safe
in our house."
A few moments later,
safe in the squirrels' house,

Alexander recovered from his fright.
How lucky he had been to fall on some trees
and to find such kind friends!
He might have hurt himself very badly.
He wanted to go to his mother
and tell her he was safe and sound.
But how was he to get down the tree?
The trunk was so smooth and so high!
A tall giraffe was passing by,
and, seeing Alexander's difficulty, said,
"Little elephant, I am going to put
my head close to the branch.

Sit between my ears and hold on to my horns.
I know your parents
and will take you home to them."
Alexander said goodbye with many thanks,
to the squirrels,
and settled himself on the giraffe's head.
The giraffe walked very gently.
"I like my pram better, all the same,"
thought Alexander. Warned of the accident by the nurse,
Babar and Celeste were already running to the spot.
What joy to find the child safe!
Arthur too was very glad.

Some months later
Babar decided to arrange a picnic.
The weather was glorious, the family in high spirits.
Cornelius got very hot,
but he managed to keep up with the others.
Hungry and tired, they gladly settled
down to a delicious lunch.

After lunch Celeste wandered off.
Babar went fishing in the river nearby.
Cornelius, stretched out in the shade, fell asleep.
Alexander took the opportunity of
creeping under Cornelius's bowler hat
and walking about, taking very small steps.
"What a funny tortoise!" said Pom.

Playing about, they reached the river bank,
and then Alexander had another idea.
He put the hat in the water. "What a fine boat!" he said,
and got into it. It floated! It was wonderful!

Then the current caught the hat and drew
it further out into the river.
Alexander was delighted with his voyage.
Pom and Flora began to feel uneasy.

How could the hat be got back?
Flora, in tears, ran to find her
mother, who was just then thinking:
"Where are the children?"
Pom ran along the bank calling out:
"Alexander! Come back!
Kind ducks, bring back my
brother, please!"
But the ducks flew away,
and all at once Pom
shouted with all his might:
"The crocodile!
Mind the crocodile!"

38

Alexander turned round. "Oh! Papa!" he screamed.
Babar was fishing peacefully.
He thought the children were playing.
But when he heard the frightened little cry
he realised that it was serious.
He stood up, and when he saw that old rogue
the crocodile, he roared with anger.

There were three seconds in which to act, and he had no gun!
The situation was desperate!
Without a moment's hesitation Babar seized the anchor
of the boat and threw it with all his might
into the jaws of the monster.
The crocodile, caught like a little fish,
in his rage lashed out with his tail.
The hat, drawn into the eddy, sank,
and Alexander fell into the water.

Babar dived in and groped about with his trunk.
He felt something!
Thank goodness! It was Alexander's ear!
Quickly pulling him to the surface,
he revived him.
As for the crocodile, he swam about frantically,
but he could not free himself
from the anchor or from the boat.

The birds gathered round Babar and Alexander
as they stood, all wet, on the bank.
"Will you do me a service," said Babar,
"by going and reassuring Queen Celeste,
and begging her to return quickly to the house
and get dry clothes ready for us
and prepare hot drinks?
And you, little ducks," he added, "will you be so
kind as to dive and bring up my crown and hat,
which are at the bottom of the river?"

Alexander embraced his mother joyfully.
She washed him, and rubbed him hard
to get him warm and then put him to bed
and covered him up with two thick blankets.
Arthur, Zephir, Pom and Flora
were still very frightened. The great flamingo
brought back the crown and Cornelius's hat.
"Oh! Thank you!" said Babar.
"The hat is rather wet and battered, but
Cornelius will be pleased
because it is an old souvenir."

Now all the elephants were asleep.
Babar and Celeste were also
soon going up to bed.
They were gradually regaining their calm
after all the excitement.
"Truly, it is not easy to bring
up children," said Babar,
"but aren't they worth it!
I don't know
what we should do without them."

46